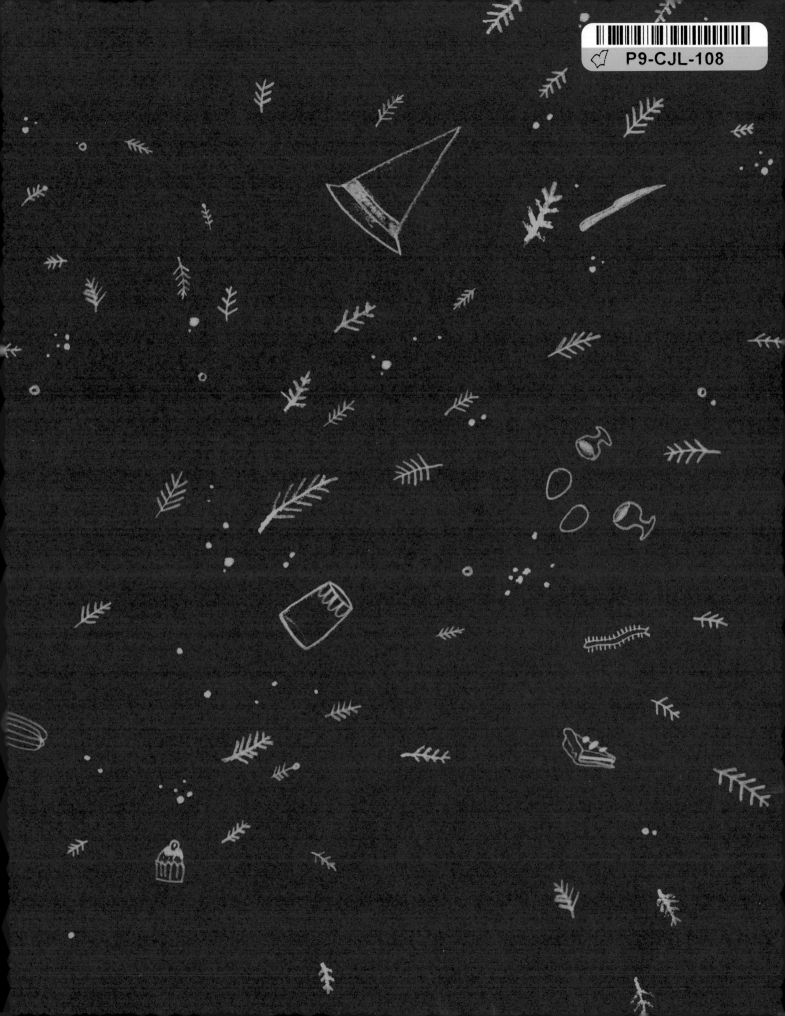

GINGRICH THE WITCH

CHEF
Recipes prepared with love.
Also caters for weddings, birthdays and christenings.

The Clearing in the Dark Woods,
To the east of the sun and the west of the moon.
gingrichthewitch@gmail.com

nubeclassics

How to Cook a Princess
Nubeclassics Series

© Text: Ana Martínez Castillo, 2017
© Illustration: Laura Liz, 2017
© Edition: NubeOcho, 2017
www.nubeocho.com — hello@nubeocho.com
gingrichthewitch@gmail.com

Original title: *Cómo cocinar princesas*
English translation: Ben Dawlatly
Text editing: Rebecca Packard

Distributed in the United States by
Consortium Book Sales & Distribution

First edition: 2018
ISBN: 978-84-946926-4-2

Printed in China by KS Printing,
respecting international labor standards.

HOW TO COOK
A PRINCESS

Ana Martínez Castillo   Laura Liz

nubeOCHO

She lives in a house made of chocolate, gingerbread and cream-filled turnovers. The roof is tiled with sugar cubes. The door and window frames, as well as the front doorstep, are made of candy canes.

Nobody really knows what her name is. Some call her Gingrich, others call her Warty-itch or just Wicked Witch. Most people prefer not to even mention her name because she lives in the darkest corner of the woods where the cold is colder, the nights are longer and the children feel more lost and alone.

In the palaces and walled gardens, where the sun shines down hard
and the princesses pick quinces, the ladies-in-waiting tell tales of
vanishing princes, huge steaming cauldrons and small boys
who never returned.

Far from the courts and royal feasts, Gingrich the witch is famous for
her delicious recipes.

There are plenty of wicked witches (every distant kingdom has one of its own), and they are all jealous of Gingrich's stovetop skills. Stepmothers and stepsisters that want to find a way to sweep a pesky princess under the rug are always asking what the secret to her success is.

Gingrich the witch's most common response is "a sprinkle of salt, a pinch of powdered mandrake and lots and lots of care." Gingrich the witch has always been a fan of a job well done.

The Art
of
Cooking Princesses

Grich Witch

KITCHEN UTENSILS

(BECAUSE YOU CAN'T COOK WITH JUST ANY OLD THING)

CAULDRON: Despite princesses often being slim, slight and light, a large, deep, nonstick pot is vital. We want to let the princess dive, belly flop and bomb from the lip of the pan and swim about freely; only then will she release all her flavor.

LADLE: A good ladle is just as important as the cauldron. It has to be made of bone or elder, and, if possible, it should have been hand-whittled on All Hallows' Eve. This is not strictly necessary, but it does give a designer twist to the stirring utensil.

OVEN: Always keep it switched on! It is our best tool for creating delicious roasts. Some advice for beginners: don't stick your head in the oven. Princesses that are on the menu often insist that we check the back of the oven, but 98% of the time it's a trap.

CAGE: It should be a considerable size. It will keep our princesses from escaping. It is advisable to lock them up with twelve padlocks and two chains. Princesses are sneaky and will always try to escape. Beware! Some are so skinny that they can fit between the bars. So it's important to feed them every half hour. We want to fatten them up, get them round and juicy so our stews have a deep, rich aroma.

HOW TO TRAP A PRINCESS

POISON APPLES: These are every cook's prize showpiece. They came into fashion a long time ago, and ever since they have been a kitchen cupboard staple. Poison pears and enchanted avocados are not without their uses. Princesses are greedy by nature, so they'll take a bite and fall into a deep sleep. And that's when we step in and take the princess home to prepare a tasty dish.

FROG PRINCES: One of the oldest tricks in the book. What we want is for the princess to believe that the warty creature is in fact a prince under a spell. The princess will kiss the beastie to try to turn it into Prince Charming. But nothing will happen, and the young royal will faint from the disgust of having kissed a slimy amphibian.

CURSED SPINDLES: As everybody knows, princesses love to sew. They can be seen embroidering quilts, sheets and handkerchiefs for their wedding night. The trick is to make the princess prick her finger on the spindle, which we will have bewitched and hidden in a secluded tower or turret for the princess to stumble across. Before we do anything, the most important thing is to hide all the thimbles!

A PIED PIPER'S PIPE: This can be very useful if the princess resists our attempts to trap her with spindles, frogs and apples. When we see that the princess is bored in her tower, we can play a simple tune. The damsel will have her glass slippers on in no time at all, and she'll be out dancing and singing without suspecting a thing. These flutes can be picked up in any magical musical instrument shop, and they tend to be well made, cheap and cheerful.

TIME TO GET BUSY!
(IT'S ALMOST DINNERTIME AND EVERYBODY'S HUNGRY)

CINDERELLA BURGER

A simple recipe for those nights when you want a bite to eat but you don't fancy hours of complex preparation.

All witches know that the secret to a great hamburger is in the bread. Wherever possible, use a bun with a few flecks of mold and some sprouting fairy toadstools. Far from ruining the dish, the fungus and mushrooms bring out the flavor of the Cinderella once she's been squished between a slice of cheese and lettuce leaf. On special occasions the cheese and lettuce can be replaced with mandrake root and eye of newt.

Don't forget to wash Cinderella properly. She's been living in the servants' quarters covered in soot and rug dust since she was a little girl. Leave her to soak for an hour and a half until all the ash has come off. And don't forget to remove her glass slippers or you'll crack a tooth!

SIDE DISHES: Roasted pumpkins, rats' tails and a handful of ugly stepsisters' toenails are popular.

ALWAYS REMEMBER: BEST EATEN BEFORE MIDNIGHT.

SLEEPING BEAUTY OMELET

The simplest things stand the test of time, and the Sleeping Beauty omelet will get us out of more than one tricky dinner-party situation. We must find a Sleeping Beauty in her natural state: in deep slumber. If she only happens to be napping, snoozing or about to fall asleep, she's of no use to us. There are stories of witches who have been struck down with food poisoning from eating a Pretending-to-be-Sleeping Beauty. So be very careful to chuck away any fakes. And if you can find one that's snoring, all the better.

Before cooking her, we must remember to pick off the eye bogies one by one. It's recommended to store them in syrup so that they can be used for spells on Walpurgis Night. The eye bogies from a princess are much sought after in witching circles. Mixed with frog spittle they have the power to make ghosts sneeze.

After removing the eye bogies from her eyes, we'll be ready to start cooking her and beating three or four eggs (make sure they're dragon eggs). It is also very important not to wake the princess before cooking her. They always wake up on the wrong side of the bed and are prone to biting.

GOLDILOCKS SAUSAGE ROLL

Goldilocks is not a member of the nobility, but she certainly acts like she is. She is fussy, spoiled and snobbish. Her favorite pastime is snooping around in other people's houses and complaining about everything. That's why we have to handle her with lots of care. She can be an irritant in the kitchen and in any other room for that matter!

First, remove her curly golden locks. The ringlets can be used to flavor soups as they have a mild chicken stock flavor. Once she is hairless and arranged on the puff pastry, season her with black pepper, add some chopped mushrooms and thinly sliced grizzly bear, roll her up and pop her in the oven. When the puff pastry has risen and the little girl has stopped grumbling, the savory treat is ready to eat.

RAPUNZEL SALAD

What's always left out of the Rapunzel story is that she was born with a radish for a head. That's why her parents had to lock her in a tower. We can, simply put, consider Rapunzel a vegetable.

This simple dish is a vegetarian delicacy for those friends of all things green and for health-conscious witches in general. With a little bit of luck we'll be able to get hold of Rapunzel's younger sister, Carlota, and add her to the salad as well. Carlota has always lived in Rapunzel's shadow, and storytellers tend to neglect her. But she was born with a carrot for a head, and her parents put her in a separate tower so the two wouldn't quarrel.

Rapunzel must first be left to soak. As the story goes, she let her hair grow hoping that one day a prince would climb her plait and rescue her from the tower. That's why we have to check her very carefully for head lice. She wouldn't be the first princess with nits. The Princess and the Pea and the Snow Queen were both reported to have lice in their hair. If she's scratching her head, we should be suspicious straightaway.

We don't need to peel Rapunzel; her skin is rich in fiber. To make the salad, just add lettuce, sweet corn, olives and tomatoes and dress with a liberal drizzle of olive oil.

SNOW WHITE STEW

This is a traditional dish that's a perfect winter's day cockle-warmer.
You will need to get hold of a plump Snow White with chubby,
rosy cheeks and pudgy arms. If you can only find a skinny one, you
will have to feed her ginger nuts for several days to fatten her up.
That said, it is quite normal to find a beautiful chunky Snow White
because she will have been living with dwarves.

Dwarves are lovers of hearty meals and sweets, and they normally inundate their guests with plate after plate of heavy food. There was one Snow White who put on 35 pounds after a single stopover at a dwarf lodge.

NOTE: THE WICKED WITCHING COMMUNITY IS VERY GRATEFUL TO THE DWARVES FOR THEIR HARD WORK IN REARING ORGANIC, FREE-RANGE PRINCESSES.

Get the stock boiling and add Snow White. When she has softened and rendered her tasty fat, add a generous handful of magic beans.

Magic beans are a delicious but dangerous ingredient. If they come into contact with soil, they can grow way up into the highest clouds where a very ill-tempered giant lives.

They also give you terrible magical wind. The smell of a magical toot from a magical bean is, of course, magical. So, if you do come face to face with the giant, don't worry, he'll probably run away in fright if you accidentally let out an otherworldly bottom burp.

BLACK FOREST RED RIDING HOOD AND GRANDMA SOUP

This recipe has been kindly contributed by my friend and master chef, the Big Bad Wolf, whose catchphrase has always been, "All the better to eat you with!"

The Little Red Riding Hoods are an excellent game meat. They are easy to find in any wild woods. At the beginning of spring, they can be found loitering around forest paths with their red hoods up, carrying wicker baskets full of snacks and skipping along to the tune that they're whistling. They are hard to catch though, as they are crafty by nature.

we will cook the Black Forest Riding Hood using the traditional
method: frying her with lots of garlic, parsley, salt and pepper.
Once she has started to brown, add a good glug of elf beer and
heat for half an hour. As Red Riding Hood has a strong flavor, she
is often served with a glass of Never-never wine.

To prepare the grandma soup, we'll need to get some water on the boil. Grannies give a hammy flavor to any bouillon, especially when they are cooked along with their walking stick. Hair rollers and nightgowns add a hot and spicy zing to the soup, so you can leave them on or remove them, according to taste. We must simmer the grandma in the broth for at least half an hour. Next, add noodles and a squeeze of lemon juice and the soup is ready to serve.

HANSEL SPONGE CAKE WITH GRETEL CUSTARD

If there is one thing that is guaranteed to have a witch greedily salivating, it is the delicate flavor of lost siblings. And they are at their best when they've gorged themselves on candies beforehand.

They are perfect for making show-stopping desserts. You can also use them to make ice cream, custard, tiramisu or trifle.

Witches often make the mistake of cooking them straightaway. My dear fellow cooks, we must never rush in the kitchen. My first piece of advice is to be neither impatient nor stingy. We ought not to worry about spending lots of money on sweet treats to fatten up the children. If you don't have a cottage made of chocolate and sugar cubes, I'd advise you to always keep a cupboard full of cookies, candy canes and chocolate bars.

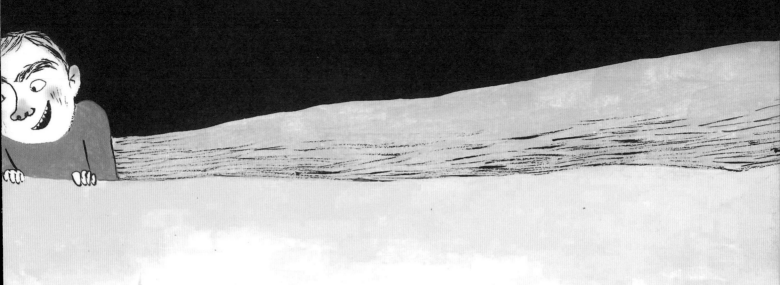

To prepare the Hansel sponge cake, first grease the little boy with butter and a sprinkle of flour. After beating a couple of dragon eggs, mix in sugar, a teaspoon of cinnamon and the zest of one lemon.

While the Hansel cake is baking in the oven, we'll prepare the Gretel custard. As greedy girls are sweet on their own, we won't need to add too much sugar. Whisk the Gretel with two egg yolks and some milk. The little girl may kick up a fuss, grab hold of the whisk or refuse to get in the pan. If that happens, the best thing to do is to tickle her with a goose feather so that she loosens her grip. It's a trick that never fails.

MORE TABLE TOP TREATS

(BECAUSE SOMETIMES WE ALL NEED SOMETHING TO NIBBLE ON)

FAIRY GODMOTHERS: These are a real treat. They're hard to find, even though they often attend royal christenings and weddings. The best examples are the wish-granting ones with the wings of a fly and a magic wand. It's easy to catch them (once you've found them); you just need a sticky strip dipped in honey. If the fairy godmother gets stuck, she'll try to bribe you by offering you a wish. Go along with it and simply say: "I wish I could eat you!"

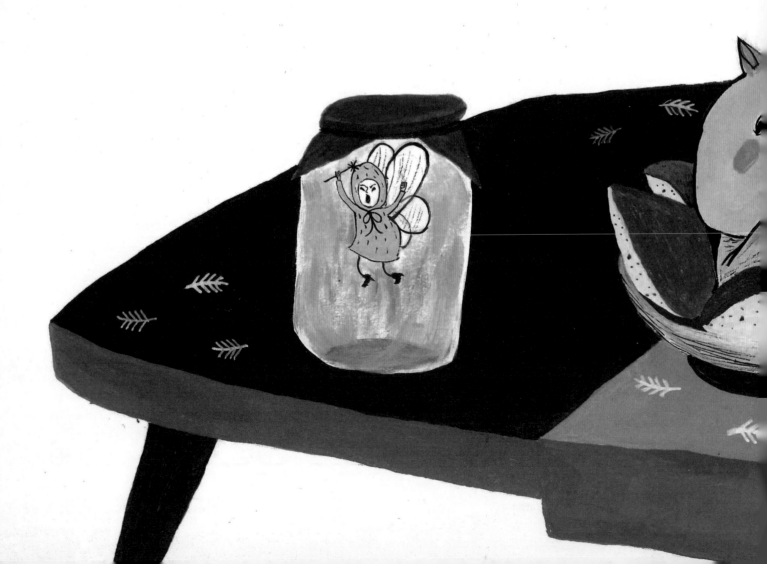

LITTLE PIGS: These are much better if there are three of them. As we all know, when it comes to pigs, nothing goes to waste, not even their houses! Pigs, by their very nature, are fans of building, architecture and interior design. Once we've had a nice roast suckling pig, we can think about moving into one of their houses built from a wide range of materials: straw, sticks or bricks. It's up to you.

PUSS IN BOOTS: This is one of the juiciest, most tender meats in the whole world. It can be used in different kinds of soups, stews and roasts. There is just one slight inconvenience: you have to wash the cat very thoroughly. The sweaty paws in those clammy boots create a smelly black gunk between the claws that can ruin a casserole. Puss in Boots should only be cooked in a large kitchen with enough room to swing a cat as that is the safest way to remove the boots.

PRINCE CHARMING: Now this is an exquisite delicacy, even more so than caviar or newts' eyes. It is the perfect dish to serve on significant occasions like Christmas, Halloween or Mothering Witch-day. We can cook him in his human form or as an enchanted frog. If the celebration is very special, we can remove half the spell and present our dinner guests a handsome prince with the legs of a frog.

Gingrich the Witch closes her opus of recipes and poses for the cameras with a look of satisfaction. She is very proud of herself, for a job well done and for the recognition she has garnered for a lifetime spent at the stove.

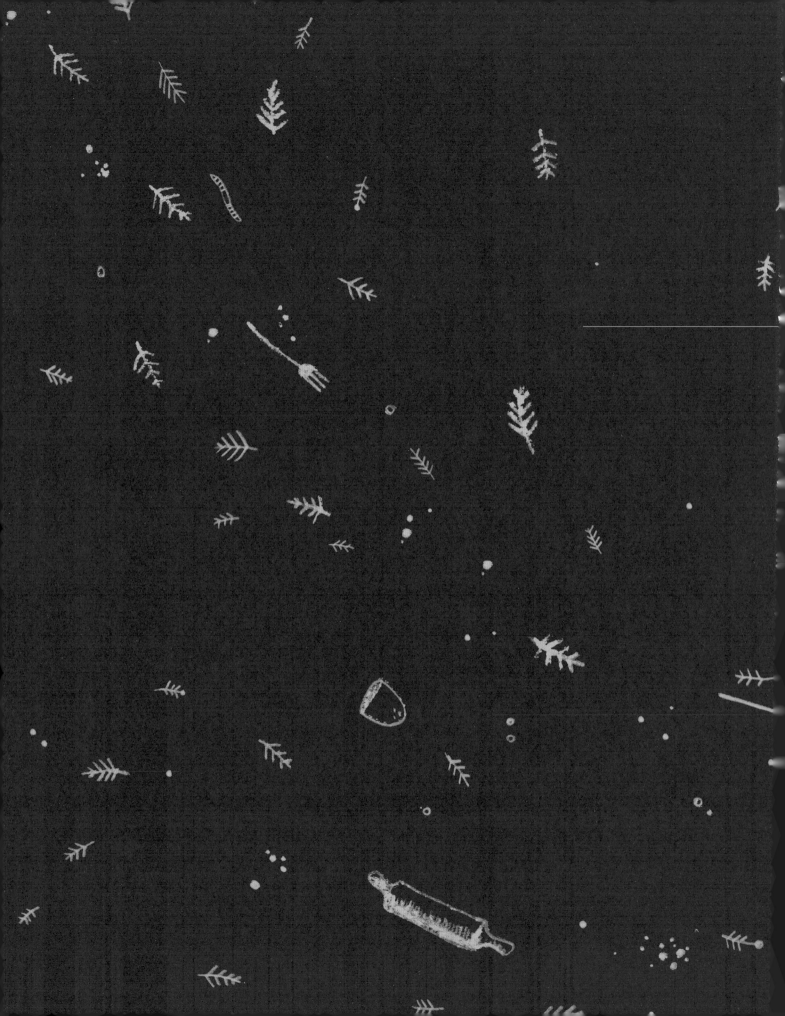